This book features . . .

a Grizzly Black Bear,

a Baby Blue Bear,

Dedicated to all the kids
who barely tidy their room.
Big bear hugs to
Genevieve and Alison.

A TEMPLAR BOOK

First published in the UK in 2017 by Templar Publishing,
an imprint of Kings Road Publishing,
part of the Bonnier Publishing Group,
The Plaza, 535 King's Road, London, SW10 0SZ
www.bonnierpublishing.com

ISBN 978-1-78370-647-1 (Hardback)
ISBN 978-1-78370-646-4 (Paperback)

Designed by Genevieve Webster
Edited by Alison Ritchie

Printed in China

YUVAL ZOMMER

Big Brown Bear's Cave

a Little Grey Bear,

and a Big Brown Bear!

t

templar publishing

One day, Big Brown Bear was taking
a stroll in the forest when he saw a cave.
It was dark and dusty and just the right size
for a bear like him.

"What a stroke of luck!" Big Brown Bear grinned.

He moved in **straight away.**

That night he tried to bear-stretch on one side of the cave . . .

Then he tried to bear-stretch in the middle . . .

Next he tried to bear-stretch on the other side.

But no matter where he tried to get comfortable, the cave just didn't feel like home.

So Big Brown Bear went for another stroll.

At the edge of the forest, he discovered something very interesting indeed.

Humans had their own caves!

The human caves were dark
and dusty, just like Bear's.
But they weren't empty.

They were full of STUFF!

There was **stuff** on the floor,
stuff on shelves, **stuff**
in boxes . . .

"I need **stuff** too!"
said Big Brown Bear.
"Then I'll have the
perfect cave."

So Bear decided to gather some STUFF for himself.

There was all kinds of stuff to choose from,
but Bear's favourites were:

stuff that came
with wheels,

stuff that came
with handles

and stuff that
came in boxes.

"I won't stop until I fill every corner of my cave," said Bear.

"My cave will have the most stuff ever!"

Word spread around about Big Brown Bear's cave.

"May we come in?" asked his friends, when they came to visit.

"I'm sorry," said Big Brown Bear, "but there seems to be
no room for visitors now, only stuff!"

Pretty soon there was no room left in the cave to even stretch or scratch or do any of the things that big brown bears generally like to do.

"Oh dear!" said Bear as he nearly tripped over box number 79.

Later on, Big Brown Bear's friends came by again.
"Won't you join us for a fishing trip?"
they asked. "It won't be the same without you."
"I'm sorry," said Big Brown Bear, tumbling head-first
into the stuff. "But I seem to be . . .

Bear's friends tried pulling him out from one side…

Then they tried pulling him out from the middle…

Next they tried pulling him out from the other side . . .

. . . until POP! at last he was free.

Bear and his friends decided it was time for all the stuff to go back to the humans.

Finally the cave was empty of all that stuff.

With his friends beside him,
Bear stretched and scratched
and found the perfect spot
straight away.

And for the very first time, his cave felt like home.